Bridge Retakes

Bridge Retakes
Angela Lopes

BookThug
Toronto, 2017
Department of Narrative Studies

FIRST EDITION

Copyright © Angela Lopes 2017

The production of this book was made possible through the generous assistance of the Canada Council for the Arts and the Ontario Arts Council. BookThug also acknowledges the support of the Government of Canada through the Canada Book Fund and the Government of Ontario through the Ontario Book Publishing Tax Credit and the Ontario Book Fund.

 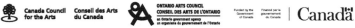

LIBRARY AND ARCHIVES CANADA CATALOGUING IN PUBLICATION

Lopes, Angela, author
        Bridge retakes / Angela Lopes. — First edition.

Issued in print and electronic formats.
softcover: ISBN 978-1-77166-302-1
html: ISBN 978-1-77166-303-8
pdf: ISBN 978-1-77166-304-5
kindle: ISBN 978-1-77166-305-2

        I. Title.

PS8623.O62B75 2017   C813'.6   C2017-900740-8.   C2017-900741-6

PRINTED IN CANADA

To our mothers

+

For Sofia and Giovanna

Phila is out in the state capital São Paulo, Brazil, to help her cousin with her beauty salon. Phila loves her family and friends in Brazil, plus she loves the food, forró and sertanejo music, and the land. She goes to Brazil at least one time every year. This time, Phila thought she'd try out a local dating site. On this dating site she met Zé. Zé posted photos of himself in his car, at his sister's beauty salon and after one of his soccer games. Zé works in a photo lab in São Paulo. Phila works three different jobs in Winnipeg, Manitoba, Canada: editing theses, cleaning and telemarketing. Her father and mother were born in Recife, Pernambuco, Brazil. Phila was born in Vancouver,

British Columbia, Canada. Zé was born in Salvador, Bahia, Brazil. He still lives with his mother and siblings, in a better favela in São Paulo. Zé's family is composed of devout Catholics with robust African traditions embedded in their daily interactions. He is extremely close to his siblings and mother. Phila's parents were raised by Phila's grandmother on her father's side and both grandparents on her mother's side. Both Phila's mother and father came from lower middle-class families. All the money they had got invested into learning English. Her mother and father met in English school at the ages of twenty-one and twenty-three. After two years of study, each working three jobs and getting married, they immigrated to Vancouver. Phila was born a year after they landed in Vancouver. Three siblings followed.

Phila decided to never forget where her parents came from, their economic struggles and spiritual suffering. Phila has little desire to buy anything, and all her savings from work go into her journeys to Brazil. She still lives with her parents in a middle-class suburb in Winnipeg. Zé has always dreamed of leaving Brazil. Zé has never ever left Brazil. He often thinks of it as a trash can. What the First World can give his family and him is economic stability, something they only get in month-long spurts, maybe two per year – a feeling of stability. Zé believes if he were ever to move to Canada to work, he could drastically improve his family's economic situation and help provide more opportunities for careers for his siblings. In São Paulo, Zé makes just enough to help out his family and finally he bought his very first car. To be approved for a Canadian tourist visa, he should own a home, have a certain amount of money in the bank, own a car and have a family that he could return home to. He only has the family and car aspects covered.

.

What if we met bigger than we fathom we are in
this disorganization?

Phila, March and April 2015, São Paulo

This age is interesting, this being thirty and all. I never thought I'd make it so far. The disorganization speaks to me at a time when I finally have some inner stability. I am always trying to understand, always trying to organize. I'm not gonna lie, I kinda like the disorganization here. It means I can organize my beginning with you. I am trying, trying to understand this disorganization. My life is getting better the closer I get to God. Here I meet Zé. Zé is a part of this disorganization, I am a part of this disorganization. Going back and forth from São Paulo to Winnipeg, twice per year, suits me. I can work in both cities. But this city São Paulo is the craziest ever. Here we get through everything and anything, so much so that all we go on is feeling. Our families are the backbone to this feeling. It may be absurd to some people, but I can no longer go on what some people say. It's not so bad that I left. We do not know my story. I remember when we walked to the car and you pulled me in, I couldn't make the next move. The car smelt of wet carpet. We wanted to stay, but we wanted to go. We bounced into the rain forest. How love can grow out of us growing out of each other. Sometimes I see you bigger than you think, like is there potential here? I wasn't sure which direction to move, all seemed resplendent. Sometimes I think I can really put it all together. Like this moment is everything with you. Like tomorrow has no matter, no place in my thoughts. I have little money because I spend it all on going to São Paulo. Sometimes I do not wanna be near you, the feeling is too robust. We are just beginning. Every time you reach out, you want to deny me. Into a must-see, must-do. I revel in the limit against what cannot be known. All my endeavours facilitate a sparser sea of flame. And if I cannot be bigger I will do more than I can, but this more is untidy. It gets ferocious. So I fabulous my eyes to a longer lash. One, two, fancy.

We cannot manage to get paid enough. To look for more work, I travel. The cleaning, telemarketing and editing are not enough. I love to engage with the people here, by any means teaching English or French or whatever. Maybe translation sometimes, too. There is something I am here that I adore, to adjoint to that family feeling. We expected nothing, I am not denying the joy in this. Being critical left us lonely, we were always forgetting ourselves, texting glamour. Every passage is vast with a catcall. But you wouldn't let me go. Our first moments together just cannot let me go. You see, sometimes my illusions are my reality, this is how I get things done. I walk differently now. All I could do was feel for you. Sometimes I didn't account for it. You gestured me where to go, and I reminded you where you're from. There is something in the water where you live. How could I leave you. But I'll be honest: my fear is that I fall drop dead in love with you, and then you leave me. I like very much being afraid. I like getting to know you, and moreover I like you telling me what to do. Every step is virtually desired. I breathed in so much of who you are, I now truly understand you. It was all so sudden.

Sometimes conceptions of webs of

thought absconding reality are the gesture to reveal it. Like my mother's phrasal structure. She gets me to do things I don't usually wanna do. But my mother is not here. It is hard to organize beyond the family here. Wild like boars, we always have something to do. They say the beginnings of love relations are too passionate. I had to put my books away to be my body. You, you just had to conquer me. And, boy, did you ever. I swear no man in Canada has moves like you. Something like wanting to be gotten becomes imperative, pastures a similar entitlement, though not a lodge in mind, rather murmurs. Did I ever tell you I know more than this? You see something virtuous now. I organize what I thought I never could. You, you are seeing me plan life, putting pieces together of our beginning.

Phila and Zé's first encounter can be encapsulated in their first kiss: slow yet with an intense beginning of love, smooth and confident. No one could tell them otherwise. It was the point where sky and ocean meet. They know very few people sense this unison. Like however they are very different, they belong together. Like it's required that they be together. It was a hot night in the state capital São Paulo. Phila's journey to Brazil this time spans two months, March and April. Phila managed to get time off work in Winnipeg. She is fortunate her jobs let her do this, as they are mostly on-call and/or online.

Phila and Zé met by the bus station. He picked her up with his car. Though Zé and Phila met online and have been conversing for almost three months, this was the first time they were to meet in the flesh. Ten years ago, when Phila was in Salvador, Bahia, for the first time, she had her wallet stolen while she was sleeping on the bus. But shortly after the experience, a beautiful man invited her to his home, fed her, gave her money and gave her his phone to contact her mother to wire some money to Salvador. Phila has never been able to forget this man, to forget Bahia.

After Zé and Phila's first kiss, in his car, a kiss that lasted for ten minutes, they drove down by the beach to have some pizza and wine. Phila could see Zé was really trying to impress her. After each having a slice of pizza and kissing a lot within a two-hour span, the waiter asked if they would like to take the rest of the large pizza home. Zé gave a flat out "no." While driving after leaving the restaurant, Zé pointed to various favelas and said, "Ó, que vergonha, ne?" Phila didn't think they were that embarrassing. She had become so used to seeing favelas; her cousin lives right beside a well cared-for favela. Phila's never lived in one, though.

Phila had no idea Zé was driving them to a motel. She had never been to one. When they approached the motel, a receptionist asked through a microphone behind the receptionist glass, "Documentos faz favor?" Phila forgot hers, but the lady let it slide anyways. Phila had no idea what to expect. Zé parked the car in a garage stall and there was a door inside the stall. The door led to a lush room, one of the fanciest rooms Phila had ever been in. A hot tub, king-sized bed, mirror on the ceiling, over 134 channels from the satellite dish, a small refrigerator with many drinks in it. Phila was not impressed. Zé was shocked she wasn't impressed. They began making love. As Zé came inside Phila, he asked her to marry him. It was a night of ascension. Nothing ever gets created without risk. Precisely because Zé and Phila didn't know and still don't know what is being created, it is creative.

What's a date?

Phila, April and May 2015, São Paulo and Winnipeg

I, Phila, couldn't work it out. I am not liking myself today.
I just can't work it out, can't put it together. I am sometimes inundated with so much felicity that I destroy. I
know my body well. I return home in heart.

Zé is an ex-
traordinary man. He's like my father; when I was born I
met him on the edge of our lineage. But is it not in our
blood to elude? I visit my parents and sometimes I live
with them. Yes, my mother submitted to divinity. She
always looks like she never wanna go anywhere. To see
is to transcend it. This leaving-behind toward an inacces-
sible total other beyond a sensible. I adored my grand-

mother's home. She never allowed me to cook in her kitchen. Her home married matter with spirit. I want to become this woman.

The winter is long and spring is being lithe. Creative ways to make money, no TV, loads of books, a Turkish carpet and the smell of sweet paprika, bay leaves and cumin. I return to drawing life, to storytelling at the university. In this, I make all the family members have a role, no discrepancy, no profligacy. Female roles are intact, male roles are far from the home. These are their only certainties, otherwise they are appeased, engaging in perhaps. Responsibilities excite them unknowingly. Hunter/gatherer tautology traversing continents. Female roles, male roles. This makes it clear. So alive, close to death.

What's a date? Sometimes I think we are too concerned with dates. Like we've gotta remember this event. It is this one marking of culture, one out of many. A silent wall of love is an invisible wall. I am certain I am foreign. That's the silent wall of love. I read because I desire to belong or I desire to lose myself, or desire because I desire loss and thus I belong. I imagine telling my family about Zé. They will hate the idea of us ever being together. I can't make peace with those that start a war with you. I see and this daggers me like tentative dates for things I really want to happen now. Sometimes I wanna live in a full house, other times I want no contacts. I actually lost my contacts. I re-meet them at work. Sometimes I remain awake at night with prayer. I believe so much of life is believing. A through-bridge. I have lived for numerous years and still have yet to be born, charity replete. This acting not for something I cannot accord, or even seeing it revolts in more me. Like this notion of going forward gets to me. I don't believe in death. I am not afraid of being my body. Lovingly rooted in my grave, I stretch out to give with little eye contact. Sentiments with sediments. We undervalue sound. The sounds of mother's voice. I cannot put a mark on this, nor attach it to numbers. Frisky yet panacea, men truly cannot be friends with me. I wanted to hide my relationship with you, Zé, for what I've always loved. And from UV rays and into our home, our dinner table. A delectable fruit that gives me so much energy. I wanted to contribute name to family. I re-experienced problems yet portions in moving between you and I on time. I wasn't sure where I found this polite awakening. My body nudged me to endeavour extraordinary. Squally effervescence in my mind sometimes so I vacate into heart. Male roles far from home. I have always known my father has regrets. This maybe is why I cannot tell my family about Zé, not just yet. Even though Recife was good to be left behind for a few years, my father always wanted to move back. Certainly we were not enough. I recall Max Weber, one foot in, one foot out. Two spheres of belonging at once. The windows were always closed in the university, some romantic egoists. Lighter than ever, I bear this pain.

All these ideas come to me while editing at the university. There's no way I can make a date for telling my family about Zé. Where would we go? My mother is my fortress, predating all. I love it when my mother penetrates me as if she knows more than my birthday. When I hide my errors, she smacks them like waterfalls on my head. Me, I love playing, still. I never want anything more than this feeling on the tips of my fingers. How to act I love you through a room of guilt when we only knew shame? As if being shy held some kinda stigma. I was never into being super social. I thrived striving to know everything. I always re-dream this. Basically my life is contagious. What I be, others watch trembling. Don't tell anyone about this clandestine drift of thought while at work. I'm not really doing anything now, but editing some thesis on the philosophy of time. As with waves, being with others excited me. So I call it a day. Where could I go? My thoughts didn't match a quotidian frame. Only friable fibs come from hearts. Just for a moment of security. What if I knew you were hiding from me? I wouldn't tell you I know, because you know I could snatch more of you. But I don't snatch.

On what day did I born. I love Phila, love myself. Will you love her more than me? I will ask this trepidation. 5 a.m. called me to work on the farm. You, Zé, said there was more to life than work, but couldn't do anything else. I only cared about where my blood came from. This severance from my ancestors is fabricated. I know them. They inhabit me when I am at the library and when with beloved in bed. The voice of all spilling all over my body. Rivers colliding, so I speak one way one day and another way the next day. I feel adored by my feet. They hold all my ancestors' respect in feeling all I know. I can handle this. Before it was too much. Now I ease in feeling too much.

As the moon blazes through my bedroom window at night. I always desire something new because I never tried to work it out with my first love. Wanting wouldn't be good enough. How one can say who one is without effort. I always want to play with my friends, being alone sometimes I was defelicitized. I like hanging out. Existentially I could handle it. My family is a part solution, part problem. They have their ways. They wanna forget where they came from, and expect I do the same. The talks about eluding city would encourage less spending was distant to us. Cash was present as a mystery. The revived desire of nothing held my spoon higher out. The dates sat on the table at the centre of a love circle. How could we replicate your harmony, oh dear one? Study, you caribou. I am turning thirty in December. I just can never be that kinda parent sitting by some pool in the sun. So let's be a lion. Being real secure, I soared today, fell yesterday. I couldn't sit still. All I was knowing came out in a tantrum tidal. The room grave in continuous check. It was the way it entered me. There is no plane on which to measure this. All I could feel was present's breathing. All the acts going around, come through. So much of life is believing and sprouting. The photo ripped through me. A scene of my family. It is time to get my life together. My parents say by this age I should know what I want. What cannot be seen nor thought. Like the microbes on this chair. A microscope can date in anti-euphemisms. Opulent palpations. Salubrious still sit here because belief is tougher than meat. My loins billow because it's simple, being everywhere every time is delectable. Like the saccharine dates on the table, I encounter you whole generations. What more can be said, except that truth is a dagger and we don't mind being cut once in a while, do you understand?

I picked guarana berries one day, united with you in the bushes. We became elusive. You knew this about me before I opened up. It is all. Yet I will howl at ill shoves. Or maybe I'll kiss them. I'll be so deprived due to calculated timelines.

The time is hard to follow. Phila read that waiting until September 6th to make a firm decision is best. There would be a series of supermoons: one in August, another in mid-September, and the last in early October. The first supermoon would take place in Pisces during Virgo's time. Zé and Phila never spoke about the moons.

Zé and Phila differ grandly with their sense of time. For Zé, it is all about the now and the next step into the very very near new. All New Age books must have learned from Zé and his family. For Phila, it is all about planning, reworking. Looking into the past to plan for the future. Their relationship is very past and future heavy. When they are together, their time is vast as the black hole. The gravitational singularity of massiveness in an infinitely small space. Space and time and density and gravity become infinite infinitely. Any secrets shared in the black hole stay in the black hole. There is no way of them getting out. Zé and Phila don't want to share too much about what they feel for each other. They know people will try to ruin it. They are not ready to face this challenge yet.

They are revelling in Maurice Blanchot's *The Step Not Beyond*, light radiating from their hearts, all of eternity in time. Sometimes it is too much for Phila to be with Zé, like she feels she will explode. Phila is back in Winnipeg, Zé is in São Paulo. Phila thinks about Zé almost all the time, checking his WhatsApp online status. Zé has thoughts of all the men who must be adoring her at present moments, and pangs of thoughts of her reactions hurt him. He knows of men who have died of jealousy. Phila is thirty years old and has a body like a horse. Call it good genes, or pure soul, but the strength that she is is what entices Zé.

They have only been intimate five times. Their bodies

knew each other before. It is too much, that feeling they have when together. Zé feels he could become whipped by the feeling of bliss. Zé is not sure he can do the distance thing.

Via long distance

Zé, May and June 2015, São Paulo

I, Zé, cannot be away from you long. Yesterday you left me. Today I am here at work at the photo lab. The retina transforms optical images, which are formed on the photoreceptors by the lens and cornea into neural image activity across myriad ganglion cells. To feel the rudiment basic thing in life is making it. I left all my memories in you where you reside. They caress me in bed or at work with all the tasks I do so well.

I will not flatter this any further. As with someone who thinks too much, I pick my cuticles. You, you think too much. It could all be so simple. The optical image is a spatial distribution of light energy while the neural image is a distribution of impulse rates representing contrast. Which is the local change in light divided by the average light level. Yesterday missed you too much. You had FaceTime on, but I didn't respond. I don't have FaceTime. Sometimes I sense felicity being away from it all. Other times grasping us all together on one way is rejoice. Every pilot needs a good patrona. A protector. The period ends here. Eyes splurge gratitude as opens the bedroom door. Sometimes you create quotes for the psyches of every actor in *The Walking Dead* on Instagram. Sometimes, Phila, your solution is to be alone. It is the silence and frequent voyages to Brazil that maintain you.

        Liberty comes at a cost. So I am saving money because I want children so badly. I evade profligacy. The transformation from light to contrast depends on retinal. I want Phila to enter on my terms. Move here with me and my family. We will have many children, we will make it work. I can't imagine another woman to be with, yet it is difficult to be with you the way things are. I will never leave my mother. She gave me life, and she is my life. She fought for me when no one had the guts. I see us together, Phila and I, and because I see it, it will be. I told her I am still living with my mother and brothers and sisters, so maybe she could feel even more for me, or wanna ditch me. Yet I will never move to her city. Let that be clear. I wanted to glue you in, Phila, but then I lost you. You so illegal it drives me into consummate explosion. We are not fearful of love, only others are fearful of us. Every day is a blessing, I can't say it any more lucid than this. And because lucid, we seek God and no other.

Truth persists as that which becomes friends get bigger on Instagram. I exude force like how we do this we do. Don't be afraid; it is not harmful, rather a panacea. Panacea as in always be true to each other. The patterned excitation of the rods and cones in the retina produce an image, and the brain processes this excitation to form a representation of. It's like that. Remember, don't be modern too much. Modern as is not traditional. Many people say suffering and smiling together, at once, what we feel for the whole. We couldn't be we with a consistent reference. Every woman in love believes in her man.

The day you came here I woke up

from a dream of a fire in the kitchen. Why does it rain every festival? All of your footprints walked in to meet you. I am an explosion of love. A desire that lives in the heart of humans. A desire to believe, moreover a desire in the other. A necessity to believe in the other, in the future, in life. Hot sex gifts are lighter than me, but that's okay. It doesn't take us long to feel something: get married and bust. The influence of pulse duration lucid in transition between multiple photon and tunnelling ionization realms. In our longer pulses photons immerse us impressionably. My landlord just governs my money from time to time. We rewire up our satellite dish and electricity for all our neighbours. Any time there is a past heavy dim light, I sob by all the busy collects a stiff neck like depression.

You have had many lovers, I fear, and I want none of them. I don't like exes. I'd like to tell you where my mother is today. She couldn't marry for love, nor for money. Doing it on the kitchen table is better anyways. Why I left for you to take on a new one, while I am still here, in love with myself? Cheating is a common experience. No silicone nor dance lessons of seduction will get me to be loyal in that regard. Sometimes you can want something so bad it never happens. The measurement uses a cavity enhanced probe of an optical cycling transition, mitigating back-action associated with state-changing transitions induced by the probe. This work establishes collective measurements as a powerful technique for generating useful entanglement for precision measurements. The photo lab is a place where there are too many tasks to do. You see, it is the little gestures that occupy my heart, need not entire but only live entirely. When we vibrate, we leave elsewhere. The orgasms are longer, like all the force on my feet. It's that felt that always takes me back to you. You that ascends me like no other nothing. Every man should dance with the woman he loves until he falls asleep. You see, there is something impossible here.

Who can enter into a relationship of love that they don't get to attend? In which they don't get to enjoy the fruit? Love knows all about the requirement of restructuring. The only way the fruit is born is to not be there.

Phila has been back and forth from Canada to Brazil so many times. Each and every time she brings Japanese and North American hair products to her cousin in São Paulo. Her cousin moved from Recife to São Paulo six years ago to open up a hair salon. Zé observes such things. He is not sure he can trust Phila: this young woman who goes back and forth from Canada to Brazil. Like, he wonders why she would want to work in Brazil. He has this picture that

Canada must be easy, so why would she want to come live the difficulty in Brazil, and work for nothing?

Zé thinks she might have a family back home: a husband and children of her own. Zé thinks Phila must be swimming in money. But this is not the reason he adores her. He adores her body. Like, it's strong like he likes it. Within the last seven months (and since Zé and Phila's first encounter), Phila has come to Brazil only one time. They have been intimate only five times. Each and every time is charged with tranquil, erotic, addictive spirit, equal panaceas for the two of them.

Phila will be back in São Paulo on September 7th. This time she will be there for three months. She has dreams of taking him to Canada with her.

Zé often asks his sisters about what they think of Phila by how he describes her. Though they like the idea that she might have lots of money, Zé's sisters say, "Nao dar certo." His sisters wonder would she really ever be able to give up the comfortable Canadian life she lives. Zé's sisters can never imagine having their brother leave them and move to another country, even if he was to help them gain more money. Compelled by his skepticism, Zé began testing Phila. He created various male profiles on the Plenty of Fish dating site and sent messages to Phila, saying all the sweetest things in the world to her. Some of these "men" even sent long poems professing their adoration of her, of her beauty. Phila never responded to any of the messages. Zé wants to know, can Phila be neglected and not run into the arms of another man? Will she stick by his side through the tough times? Will the issue of class eventually bother her? Is this just a casual fling? Will she move to Brazil to be with him without him having to ask her?

At an Umbanda gathering there was, as always, lots of smoke. Umbanda is a blended spiritualist movement that involves African traditions with Roman Catholicism and Indigenous peoples of Brazil's practices. Phila felt delight losing herself in the smoke. A man wearing a long white tunic and beige pants, she swore was Zé. The way this man moved, the way this man stood, the way this man hummed. But Zé would never in million years go to an Umbanda gathering; he is a devoted Catholic.

47

The drumming and chanting were getting more intense as people approached healers, seeking advice for the events and ongoing of their lives. The avó wore a white shirt and loose fitting jeans. The food on the floor in the centre of the main room: cicada, farofa com carne secs, and coconut water. Candles lit everywhere on the side tables and the floor around the food. People were standing all against the walls, mostly the men (though there were only five) and women, but most of the women were sitting, some younger women sitting on other women's laps. The scent of tobacco smoke everywhere. One man there asked Phila, "Where are you from?" Phila replied, "Canada." "Muito chic," he replied. Phila approached the avó and asked her questions about Zé. The avó said some things that Phila didn't really like. The avó said, "It will not work as a traditional relationship."

Phila asked an avó to join her in prayer for Zé and her to be together. The avó said their relationship will not work if they live far from each other for too long. It will be fine for them to live apart for a year or two, but any more will be too trying for them. She felt spirits enter her, spirits of calm. In particular, Naná: the supreme mother, mother of the moon spirit and the sun spirit. They reminded her of Tapa, as in reflection. Tapa is getting to second thoughts and not merely being satiated with the first appearance of something. When really searching, we see that the entire universe cannot be looked upon as mere chance.

Are you ignoring me?

Phila, April, May and June 2015, Winnipeg

Cannot be looked upon as mere chance. Let me distinguish for you the difference between the letters A and B. Together they show us optional points. One follows the other, the other precedes the one. When chanting the alphabet, without B, C cannot follow. If you are A, let's say, and I am B, shouldn't I follow you? Or maybe it's the other way around. But either way, not mere chance.

When people tell us no, we say most certainly yes. I will organize this confusion, this disorganization. Like what are our roles for each other, duties for each other? All the thoughts swimming in your mind that are eating away at you. Away at you and me. Don't you see I need a good man to well for. Sometimes you can want something so bad that it happens never. Me, I adore transforming every bad experience into a good one.

Why are you ignoring me? I remember what the avó said at the Umbanda. I trust what she said. So many things are not said here. Like, why can't you tell me directly that you want me to stay with you? We say it is winter here and the landscape view is every difference just taking some getting used to. São Paulo's winters don't compare to Winnipeg's. There are variables of gas, dust and air. You test me. Are we not sure who should follow and lead? Like a good kinda wife will not nag you notoriously with an inundation of text messages. Not sure how everything is turning out. Yesterday I walked to the ocean, yet we live five hours from it. My walk comes from my ancestors, grandmothers vivified more than my mother. Almost every second day, they cut our water off. What will they scold our generation for today? See fortitude, but finances non-existent. And I only really have a fear of God. There are tents here that hold up everything, all my friends comfort shelter. Our lives are such astonishing ventures within each and every one of us. Most Americans need an answer right away. Like, why are you ignoring me?

Now I wanna talk about directness. The point of the matter is that people will always talk. This is something you can't run away from. To gabber all one can muster. You, you like silence. I like you. Why didn't you answer my text message yesterday? What's never speaking to you mean then, all of a sudden I'm essential? You left me drawings all over my notebook. We play dating games together. You are the largest player telling me things I wanna know. It may look desperate if I go out with you last minute. That I like being lost. You called me to check up on me, but from a different number, yet I know it was you. The way you play gets into me. I like very much to know you're giving me genuine. Like a heart hitchhiking into a mind. I love everything about being alive and this orgasms me into another you. Ignoring those you love only goes so far. Tomorrow will be a better day.

You, are you embarrassed to take me to meet your family? As you ejaculated in me, you asked me to marry you. Why do you avoid me now? Why we bleed for days after. Our families meeting in our bodies makes me love every-man-I-love's mother. What about the other woman? Sometimes she can be a friend. If cheating is not wrong, if more vitality returns domestic. How wanting you more meant not touching you for days. Our bodies we never neglect to recollect. My actions victim possessive these jeans as skinny as they are. A woman just has to give space, that's all. I want straight answers and my family is everything. My sister lets go and still we unite, this is family. People become direct for primal urges. I need children, not want but need, like, four. Women can share duties. I am not afraid of introducing men to my children. They will adore them, of this I am sure. We want children together. Why let this be need be minuscule? It is not. I need you to impregnate me.

On WhatsApp your status is lucid. Did I ever tell you you are my favourite lover? What did you walk through when I crossed my legs? But the whole selfish thing rocks me, like shouldn't people be replete? Implementation calling me selfish, but I adore myself. And even more so, I adore everyone. I feel tranquil alone at the metro. I still want to have your children. Why do you ignore me not answering my texts?

Yesterday I met Zé for lunch in a motel. I revel in teaching lessons. Like these feet are surreal, I swear. A reverie is all but the aforementioned. Lover, why did you not call me after you asked me to marry you? I swear I'm fortified. Everything brings me closer and I can tell when you're pulling my G-strings. So I let you be and you spirit me, asking ejaculation even more often into me. The norms of this circumstance get eradicated by love, you see, I'm not of trepidation of you. But they will ceaselessly crumble. And one plus one is one. Not of us. Ginger of our dignity. We only fear one thing so big. I want my children smart, happy on the inside – a smile or not, it's all in the heart. My sisters are this earth, must be gentle and love each other. A man must not give much of himself, that she pines for it, but this thing is love itself. All my children will be growing too robust, this world turns celestial. This is another time.

Because of the suffering, people play games. It is the crime and rising costs that are the only deterrents. If we retrieve a short chance from some lives I can live in a mansion or a ditch. The intelligence of the heart is all I call home in each of you all. They can't see this, how could they? There's some emergency here. I hold the money for us. We fated a marriage to feed your family. Why are shops open when no one is here? Me, I don't buy, little stealing too. My ex can't be my friend if you enter my life, you see. Like the last one who proposed marriage to me couldn't get away. My breasts are tender today. Kegels I maintain ritual. Doing things as a couple is boring; I prefer mother, children, sisters, grandmothers. The fixed bourgeois relation a priori excludes fresh air. This time I marry you and only you eternity. No longer norms present. Each quote is a dance floor.

Today it rained for three hours. We must be together tonight. Every reality for me is how I imagine it, it gets patient, it gets radiant. You never invited me to your house. Why trust in an elastic band. Yesterday I visited my cousin's place. Her heart is all over the place, walking 500 feet into the ocean. We are not hunting for we can never bait. My impulse is to have five children with you. As we are growing up, they are finding us more attractive. My sister said, "This guy better not be playing you." But that's not how family works, striking rapid blessing not replete beget. See, you gotta work for it. How could they understand? I'd rather do whatever you ask me. I read that for a man to warrant his security, he needs to stand distance. This obscure for a modern mind. We meet always when the calling. I knew you before you called. You see what I'm saying: it's a rich life and we have no house. Being too serious makes me vomit. May we play all avenues first. Everything about you exhilarates me to run to you. Yesterday I dreamt of a leaf and a lion and your mind.

What do we do when we will die for our parents?

Every day is a grind, but what is outlandish is divine. I am ignoring my work today. Some difference between belief and gratitude. Like if I work so hard to get in. I'm it, with spirit. There is nothing more splendid. Since I can't sleep I go to storytelling. In telling all I intend to know. Where you capture me, I'm bounded by your thigh. I cannot sleep. But where are you?

Ignoring someone is one of the oldest forms of punishment. Zé has been ignoring Phila for over a week and a half. She sent over six messages to him, and he has yet to respond to any of them. The last time they were intimate was in April. It's a pity that when Phila is in São Paulo, Zé doesn't have a place for them to share together. Phila stays with her cousin and Zé always lives with his family. It would be a great disrespect to his mother if Phila stayed with them. Besides, Zé is too embarrassed to have Phila see where he lives – it's too early for that.

Phila left São Paulo and returned to Winnipeg at the end

of April. It's hard to keep track of times and dates. She wants to talk to Zé, but he is ignoring her. Phila often imagines she is in São Paulo. She gets delusional, thinking she's still there. Friends notice this about her. Two close friends advise her, "You need to know when to say goodbye." But Phila thinks Zé is testing her. Maybe he is insecure about his economic status because he cannot provide for her in the way she is used to in Canada. His family thinks she has a husband in Canada, thus lying to him about being single. This certainly influences Zé tremendously. He can't fully see the value in waiting for Phila. Life is short and survival means staying close to those you love. Proof of a woman's love is abandoning all to be with her man.

Ever since Zé met Phila, he has wanted to impregnate her. Ever since Phila met Zé, she has wanted to have children with him. This subconscious decision is what keeps them going. Despite the fact that Zé hates how Phila comes and goes to São Paulo, there is the very basic desire to procreate together. And it is this very basic desire that is in unison with so many higher virtues to practice and extend upon: humility, compassion, love.

Phila refuses to give up and sends messages every day. She suffers in silence, only telling two friends – her cousin and her sister, Camila. After ignoring her for a month and a week, Zé found out from her WhatsApp status that she would be going to Ceará with her cousin on September 7th. Then he came running back to her with a fountain of messages.

Crossing that bridge

Phila, September 2015, Ceará and São Paulo

With a fountain of messages, you know you want me, Zé. Why were you away for so long? Do you know what you did to my heart, do you? You know you could never miss the chance to not ever see me again. I am moving on. You heard I would be away for a while. You sent me a text saying, "You're not gonna cheat on me, right?" So when I'm at the beach all I can think about is you. Now you got what you wanted. Everything here in Ceará is unessential. The only being essential is you. Shouldn't a man at your age know what you want by now? Every woman wants stability. Not knowing what is to come is even more thrilling. I adore everything I don't understand.

Today is the day we attention our future children. Look, if we have many, our children will care for each other, care for us. Look how your love savours good. Everyone at home is asleep and here we are. I'd rather these words not signify something, rather bring you somewhere you really wanna go. You say you'd come to Canada for me, but I fear for some of your boredom. We had to leave our presence for all the bold things to happen. In your WhatsApp message you said, "It's all gonna work out, I miss you." You and I never use condoms. Why would we? I will marry you one day and we will have between three and six children. Your heart is soft, yet your body is strong. I can never tell you you did wrong, though, you would get really mad. Telling you what to do would mean setting myself up for a big fight. You are fiery, how I like my men. You never want me to be critical of you. You never want me to be close to any man other than you. But what the heart doesn't see, the mind doesn't know. You wanna mark me as yours. The beautiful primal necessity to deposit one's sperm into the woman of a man's dreams. Where blood pumps life, never giving up until worn.

Whether a new event is greeted with hope or cursed as a dark fate may depend not entirely on whether it is good or bad but also partly on the inner attitude of the person to whom it happens. Love is like that, too; every lover comes first as an unknown stranger and promises a woman both great joy and great danger. I only want to get to know people who live long and full lives. And all the people that also suffer from a lack of life, I want to know as well. I see, closing my eyes, a vision of what will be my reality, and this is it. I want my children travelling with me.

I wonder about this intense feeling to reproduce, this very primal and crucial push. I love everyone, but the feeling to want to have a child with someone one loves is the best feeling ever. I am sure if I get pregnant, I can secure anything in life. But to necessarily secure a man, I am not craving. Securing my body and my babies' futures, their education, their health and well-being, is always my mission. I don't want reality. It robs innocence. A selfish mother doesn't let her children be with any other woman. She fears they may like the other woman. I will die from so much love, my blood radiating through my body ascending floors.

Today I'm going to a party. You, Zé, always stay with family, how you like it. Why are sesame seeds so sexy scattered on this table. My lover's seeds are in need. Men walk firm here in Ceará, caress my face, pinch my cheeks the coats of crime. Levi's jeans clenching me or a man's hand ravenous, I believe. There are games that men play to hold secure. Remember the night you took me to that motel? All night silence as dengue mounts populous. I know too much this time. I am persisting with nothing, anything knows so much is squirting. I can only lie for so much. My body is too good for me. Pardon me for taking so much of a span, just making sure you will not run out on me and our future children. What about the games men play to see if she's sincere. We can never ever juggle silence here. Too much static. If you call me tomorrow, I will go out with you, if you ask me, do these things take so long. Everyone has a care in the world for a moment in time. Which makes us crave our real friends. A city of people in heat. Of workaholics that work the labyrinth metro like a third job. Where children seem to only play indoors. Where we make love hard for moments, and then fight the next moments. Where the group and the mother are bigger than any skyscraper here. Where almost everyone is cheating and egoism is high, yet everyone is determined to make their lives work for themselves, for their families. However, the modern woman is hitting hard here. The men in this country are the flyest I've ever known. Eyes and hands. What a party. My sister, she needs me so I pick up my cell and dance to her.

This morning's smog is a sultry disposition. I am thirty years old and time works under the table. To make something from what my heart knows. To know what's right, what's wrong, outside the system. The avó said being separate from you will not work for longer than two years. After the Umbanda ceremony we had fevers of a hundred. Guys sometimes want what they feel is too far out there for them. But when they do have it, they still pine for more. You haven't called me in over a week. I play it like a pro. We ruminate about problems and people and how to tell if a woman is really good. Our tablecloth is a consummate union of our bodies. I was told to just move on. Why is that painting exhibiting a faucet with drops of water and people holding umbrellas? So I walk this decision, or read all shop signs. The protests are taking over. And I don't miss my returns to Winnipeg. To decide comes from Latin *dêcîsio*, a cutting off. I am not a fan. Derrida meets decision with loveance, "passive," delivered over to the other, suspended over the other's heartbeat. Where I am helpless, where I decide what I cannot fail to decide, freely, necessarily receiving my very life from the heartbeat of the other. We will have a baby one day soon enough. This will be the most stunning day.

The protests continued every day after 4 p.m. Change will be where I work, and it's no surprise I do where ends meet. Most of my friends are either artists or not born in North America. They are my blood. I miss the parties with them. Yesterday night I put 60 *reals* into my bra before I met you. Today I will put in 40. Not sure why you forgot. As a storyteller there is that feeling you don't know what you're doing with your life. Like everything takes forever. Why we neglect things that are sorta essential is something I occupy time with. Scattered among the superfluous I enriched a body like none other. Logic obnubilates my heart, then

I feel I can no longer live. Sometimes the right time to go is never-ending as you secrete behind your cell only messages you receptive to obtain. Some things take so long to happen.

People will always talk about us because we're too beautiful. After you closed up the photo lab with your co-workers, I met you outside your work. We walked avenida Paulista. A change is needed here, as it is with us. We don't know what this means. Don't be fooled by my the short shorts and belly tops; I don't put out easy here. We watched the protestors, we walked on our own.

Everyone is ready for a change. Everyone is tired of the corruption. The disgust that the upper class is. Tired of how the possession of nature is the aim for the sneaky ones. The obsession with security and the disgust with anything that is against it takes life away. A need to be together that only makes sense being far apart. Where will Phila's family find the sense in her relationship with Zé? Society may never accept them, not that they care, but their families' acceptance is important, especially for Zé.

Phila cannot tell her family. Sometimes remaining silent about one's story can be the most liberating feeling. That to only talk about one's story when one knows more about it will lessen the jinx potential. Phila resents that her family in Canada, with parents born in Brazil, never send money to her family in Brazil. Phila's parents have a fairly good family business. They buy all kinds of gifts for their family in Canada, but have chosen to forget all about their family in Brazil. After all, they feel, what did Brazil do for us? After all, they feel their siblings are not without money. Her parents have lost the group consciousness that Phila pines for. That when one individual in the family is suffering, we all are. Happiness is only real when shared. Phila's parents think the social custom of kissing on both cheeks is fake.

According to Zé and Zé's family's perception of Phila, she too lacks this group consciousness. They all feel, based on everything Zé has shared with them, that Phila is experiencing the high life in Canada. She is not perceived as some angel saving Zé and Zé's family from economic strife. She is perceived as selfish and not serious about Zé. She is perceived as not truly loving him. Zé really needs her body and feels that his family can benefit from Phila and her situation. The feeling of freedom Zé gets from

Phila is tantalizing. Money can open the door outside of Brazil's class system.

Phila, out of adoration for Zé and to show him and his family she is serious about him, starts sending him money when she is back in Canada. She wants to build a life with him, and thinks it is a sacrifice to be at a distance in order for her to save money and send money to him. Yet at the same time as having this feeling that she wants to build a life with him, she has some doubts, and she is profoundly worried that her family will never accept Zé and her pregnancy. According to Phila, this is not the right time to move to Brazil. Zé thinks that even though Phila is sending money to him, Brazil is always having an economic crisis and she should still move to Brazil to be with him, if she truly loves him. Phila has pangs at the thought of how money can confuse love, how it changes subject matter. The notion of security is a muddle for them. Zé thinks Phila does not need him to feel secure in life. He knows Brazil is for the strong.

Phila thinks from time to time (especially now as she has listened to a few friends tell her "be careful, he may be using you to get to Canada") that Zé may be using her. But Zé and Phila don't dwell in these kinds of negative thoughts too long. Phila is pregnant. What good would it do to be under the influence of many people's negative thoughts? Both Zé and Phila honour the space of the grey. For Zé, Phila is his most preferred woman, no other can compare, others just satisfy spontaneous feeling. For Phila, Zé is the one. Zé refrains from talking about Phila and their relationship to extended family. It is enough that his immediate family knows. When too many know, many will try their hardest to ruin a good thing. Phila entrusts her current life with her friends, her cousin, her sister Camila, and listens to some people at the Umbanda. Her family will not be able to handle all the new changes coming their way. Phila cannot tell Camila everything, just some details. All she can say is that the English school she works at in São Paulo is great, their family is great, and she loves the beaches.

The bridge opens to ideal as real

Phila, September and October 2015, São Paulo

After reading Paulina Chiziane, I saw women. The women in Northern Mozambique are the best women. They have many children, and they are the most beautiful mothers ever. They are so confident. What's stopping me from being this kinda woman? I knew we were pregnant the day after we conceived. Our lovemaking that night was over the top. Sometimes I wonder how the body knows, like I could feel this tiny ball moving along a small pathway in my uterus. I couldn't think of anything more stunning than having a child. Let's just say we are entering a new epoch. The day I thought I was pregnant was the day I received a call from the university saying that they needed to cancel my future contract with them. That contract was to start nine months from now. Sometimes I enrapture myself secretly, believing I am better than the modern woman. I never feel competitors; what would they look like? Fuzzy, lint-ridden, then disposable. You, Zé, are all I need from a distance and sometimes too close when we are together. I remember when you grabbed me from behind on the escalators in the subway system and said you're all I need. Everything about having a child right now simultaneously terrifies and thrills me. I am trying to remain calm, trying to remain calm. That you, Zé, are far, is not a concern for us right now. I let the source of my intuition weave abstractions, because as we know, the heart is truant from no fragment of the sky, just as it is truant from no vein in ourselves.

I think of the women in Northern Mozambique in Chiziane's book *Niketche*. The women have so many children, yet still maintain stunning figures, gorgeous on-point faces. They run their communities. They live in a matriarchal society. Giving birth is a blessing. Feminine, not feminism.

Sometimes I spend all my spare time thinking how such an event can occur. And how it occurs so often. How little we value it, sometimes. The atoms of our pact evacuated some strident I that I could no longer be. Like before I spoke about how this whole selfish thing rocks me. There's a balance that is needed. Like care for the self, care for others, care for the self, care for others. I care too much for everyone that this births me into everyone. What I wanna be currently is selfness opulent riotously emitting itself. Like the women in *Niketche* sharing their men. Like the women in Northern Mozambique living matriarchal. The empathy current is a feeling, an undoing what was doing listening for hearing. Whenever I have money, I give it away. Scathing saccharine streets extend wanting another language to grow up in, all senses reconvened with ethics. I really have much to do, but I need my body still. I say body still, but what I mean to say is indwelling of simultaneous dormancy and nascence. There is nothing more radiant than getting up at 4 a.m. with a resurgence to tell a story. There is little work for me to do. Like everything comes when needed and all will be fine.

Like everything comes when needed. This is good enough. Phila's present of perception, joy of life and imaginative utopian matriarchal futuristic vision are extraordinary. The boundaries are blurred betwixt languages and creativity and experience. She gets confused sometimes passing through a high degree of love. The role of woman is relative to how Phila wants it, to how she necessitates it, to how she observes her role models.

Work serves a purpose for Phila to afford travel and buy material wants. But work for Zé is essential. Work in many regards. Zé feels men lose their power when they cannot provide for their women. Why would a woman stick around for long if her man cannot provide for her?

Phila never wanted to be a career woman. She always wanted to find the right man to follow. Zé always wanted a true housewife. Zé always wanted the perfect woman to obey him. Both live with their families. And Zé wants so badly for his family to meet Phila, but she must commit to him. She must be serious and devoted to only him.

In my place

Zé, September and October 2015, São Paulo

For me to be in my power, you gotta let me work. I read on Facebook someone quoted from their Introductory Physics book: "The beginning of the time of inflation left the stunning universe behind, space today is replete with invisible fields moving rapidly across space, gravity and dust bringing up matter." I'm Catholic; science can only say so much to me. Inflation knows nothing of well-being. But you, Phila, stirred everything in my being the moment we met. You are too strong, in many regards it terrifies me how some of the freedom you have is so money dependent. And some of the freedom you have is from abandoning fear, so much like you were born in my family in Bahia. With you I feel a rush resplendent right. I'm thrown off my element when I have no work. When you're in Bahia with me, I tell you where to go. But here in São Paulo, it's as though the women tell the men where to go. The competition is fierce and women never learn how to cook here. I love women, but when they talk too much I get irritated. But you, Phila, are different. I gotta get you to depend on me for money. You North Americaners are too naive. You all think we want your lifestyle. We want to be like you. Thank God, Phila, you are different. You enjoy your life always, anyway and any means necessary, while I am here in São Paulo. Remember that our love may too be a roof for our heads. You catch my drift. If you move in with me, I can please you. Soon you will deliver lightly the news to your family how touch can act on everyone, or beat the meat to your thoughts. It is hard to transmit my intense feeling for you through these technological devices. Like how to say I love you through this handheld thing. Yesterday you told me you want me more and more each day. The lasting of nothing so far. We are not going to be recovered because we are here, you and I. To retake all that is of our lives with us. I've had it. Yet still, you must move here to truly be with me. There is no other way around it. It is in your name, Phila, love. Love is a kinda condition to happiness surpassing all transactions and the system of work. Beyond price, it promises transcendence. But modernity questions absolutes. Like how the man's role is dominant. Phila, you understand this. Phila, you are different. You don't try to possess me. But sometimes I wonder, do you really love me? Shouldn't women wanna be by the one they love like, all the time. But anyways, I love you more than any needy one. I want you by my side. It is certainty with a veil.

It is certainty with a veil. There is nothing more gorgeous than to be certain of something in our lives. But the pain of feeling that while simultaneously knowing that other loved ones don't see the gorgeousness of this particular certainty is difficult. The words that Zé and Phila share together via long distances are not enough.

For Phila, possession comes through abstaining. She feels best giving liberty to Zé. If Zé is to move out of his family home on his own, away from his mother, he needs a good woman to live with. Whatever happens outside the home always stays outside the home.

Whether occurrences such as the ones Zé and Phila have been sharing are accepted with the warmth of faith or shuddered with the cold of dismay depends on the inner workings of the individuals there to receive it. The warmth is in their hands.

Why spirit and for spirit and by spirit, are all things

Ze and Phila, December 2015, São Paulo and Winnipeg

We read a message on WhatsApp saying that it helps a pregnant woman to remain calm if her man is present, at least like once a week or something. We saw it on a psychology website. His DNA in her creates sentiments of attachment to him. We miss each other's caresses, which secure us like none other. That from caresses we cross bridges and invest all spiritual energy into the raising of our future children. Today could be the day we tell everyone about us, but no. Our families can't meet, two oceans with land between them. To our blessedness, we don't let that perturb our relation. We keep open because it best suits us. We never let family drama affect us too much. We are close to our parents, our brothers and sisters, yet we know our boundaries. Virtue is well known to us. We can only speak of who we are. That ever since we were born, we go with a different kinda time. We wonder if our family and friends ever tried that dating site. We know from some shared stories that yes, they did. We love one another's voices and the pollution is too much here. We, we adore nothing more than spirit where it snags the richest eradication. A feeling of needing nothing more than us together. Where did we go last night during our Skype talk? The future is luminescent, so we adapt to light, to whatever comes tomorrow. That night is all because too much security makes us vomit. If we're kinda the jokes in the family, it's because our hearts don't settle on status. We rip standard pedagogy into an ocean surf of octopus caught cleaned out. All the time we are malleable in pastures. There's that ravenous explosion vivifies us into stellar amour. Inoculated by the system's lies, we become wealthy with integrity, so much that they can't see us. Every morning we get up stuffed to give. Every graze and subsist makes us diligent about meaning. Things could get better after this recession that we die for us on top of matter is all we've got. The push/pull is a beginning thing, it turns a tiring shrug. We're past our beginning, past the game-playing. Please don't omit the opening of all time that may be. If there is anything we do before going to sleep, it is pray to all the salt water. We swim eons for sentiments of nature. And, yes our bikes carry coconuts for fifty people as we sojourn all parts where people speak to us. We listen well to people, but more to each other. Every morning appears a lagoon. Many opted out of the Cartesian split, making an island, careening the fortitude of belief's thick delight. We know this life gets all the asking and more. The Internet connection sucks, so we launch reticence and spunk. We walk to the *aqua doce* and wash our clothes in the river. Every nude video we send to each other is fine, but we know we want the real thing. Everywhere we go we are each other, there is no other pace. Did other people ever try the taste of trust? Our breakthrough performance is, what's my body without yours? Snared by subterfuge over the corruption crackling. Anything we do makes us want to do anything we want. To us it doesn't matter where we go because we are in us not surprised that we fell. Why crave a roof when we've got our ancestors. We never followed the white way.

My nipples are extra sensitive today and you touch them. Tornado touch is a semiotic svelte getting whatever exercise at work. Today is the day we will spend all our saved money and we will get good food and not think about the future. Only of our children, of their future. Sins to dishonour the body collect vile affections in cell. We elude responsibility because spiritually it numbs. A brush of the chair and we're all over our relationship. Sometimes we get our history and other times we churn out the brisk banishment. To suffer is what years our branches. Why feel fresh when pollution enters our thoughts from history in the making, we tempt nothing grand. Will we please hold us together forever, only to let us go.

Phila is back early for Christmas in Winnipeg. So much reality and reverie. Camila picked her up at the airport. Phila has been away from her family in Winnipeg for over three months. Camila is not impressed. While they were in the car leaving the airport, Camila asked sternly, "Phila, what are you doing with your life?" "I'm in love, in love like I've never been." "Oh God." Phila shared with Camila her experience of Umbanda. How the orixás had entered her and will never leave her. Camila listened to all of the words, but is not happy. "Don't you just want me to be happy?" asked Phila. "Why can't you just be happy with us, your family, here? Why do you have to keep running away?" Phila shared an experience she had with Zé on one of their dates. A feeling she received that she'd never had before: a feeling of wanting to heal another being. One time, she told Camila, when Zé went to watch a soccer match, his team lost. Zé was holding a glass cup in his hand when his team let in the winning goal, and he crushed the glass and cut his hand deeply. Zé met Phila after the game at a café, and when he told her about his hand, she grabbed it and licked off the remaining blood, went and asked the server for peroxide and Band-Aids. Camila looked concerned. She had never seen Phila like this, ever.

Phila never felt right being back. She knew she would have to cease working the cleaning job. That kind of job would be no good for a pregnant woman. Continuing with the telemarketing and thesis editing at the university could be sufficient for the time being.

After Phila fell asleep in her bed, Camila stayed up late talking to their parents. "I'm gonna go with Phila next time to São Paulo." Their parents are worried. They want Camila to go with Phila next time. Their parents don't want Phila to know that they are as concerned as they are. Already, Zé has sent six WhatsApp messages to Phila. They spend Christmas apart this year. But next year, who knows.

Phila and Camila are off to São Paulo at the end of January. Phila is not sure what the answer is. She and Zé just need to be close from now onward. Zé believes too much in their chemistry, in their truth. Phila sends messages to Zé about the simplicity of the black holes in the oceans of his home state, Bahia. The eddies that pull you in are like photon spheres. Zé can't swim. So whenever they go to the beach, Phila swims. Zé watches her in amazement. They dream of swimming together and they do.

Phila is excited to bring Camila to an Umbanda party. The party coming up in February will celebrate Iemanjá, queen of the ocean. Camila found an Umbanda house that will celebrate Iemanjá in the capital São Paulo. Phila has never been, nor never heard of this place. Though Phila feels it will not be an authentic celebration, she agrees she will try it out. After all, Camila is making great effort to connect with her.

For a while, Phila has felt that Camila needs some spiritual healing, while Camila feels Phila needs a reality check. But what's more is that Camila made a promise to their grandmother, right before she passed away in Recife, to always take care of her little sister. Phila's always been centred in the heart chakra, but within the last year or two she's been even more centred there, so much so that Phila attracts anyone and everyone. Even getting work is easy for her. The cleaning job she had to let go. Though she was making good coin working the hours she did with the cleaning company, inhaling the products would be no good for a growing being in her. The telemarketing job is practical. She can ditch it whenever she needs to, return to it whenever she needs to, though it is soul-wrecking. Like, she feels the depression slowly seep into her like sewage. It's a temporary solution.

Phila ought to just move, to be with Zé. She's asked him a few times: when will I meet your family? He keeps saying, when you move here, you will meet my family. Phila is scared to run out of money. This thing that determines so much, reveals so little yet so much. A house full of beauty.

Can't keep running away, to Iemanjá

Phila, February 2016, São Paulo

A house full of beauty. Some things are a little fake. But next year, who knows, from the perspective inside the black hole, this is secret. From an oceanic perspective, it's a secret kept. The black hole can never communicate with anyone outside of it, not even an ocean surf. Secrets safe forever. This early January I have been working 55 hours per week. You are with me. Taking adventure. All my runnings are to you. I recumb, listening to The Pharcyde's "Runnin'" in my bedroom, scheming a way to make money fast. Let's continue our crazy lush together. The light is our adventure as it hits our green-blue ocean. If ever I walk, I'll never get there. I am protective over you. I caress you with strength runnings with a wave of security from heart salt. The truth of the matter is, I don't like you around anyone else but me and your mother and your sisters. When I look mathematically, all ocean eddies are black holes. Nothing and anything in them can ever escape. You and I, we attract everything that gestures relatively close to us. You move around in closed loops, in oceanic like a photon sphere. Anytime we go to the ocean, we are taken in. A collapse of dead stars in our oceanic communication. Did you ever get sucked in there? But I swear the photon light around such intense gravity holes does us in. I fathom our baby surrounded by that photon light. This all serves as a kinda motivation during Winnipeg's harsh winters. You, you are always working. Sometimes I think the photo lab ought to be occupied by photos only of you. Photos all over the lab, of you, only you. The next Umbanda gathering will involve me chanting you. I see it now. Chanting, because what else can come out of me, but you. I've kept you from most of my family for too long. Everyone knows amour. Love, I am dying without you. I trust her too much. Let this be clandestine. I remember we went

in the ocean, we got pulled in. I will never forgive anyone that ever hurts you. And I promise, our children will
always be in good hands.

Living off of little or plen-
ty, let's go to Umbanda. I recall the avó saying, "Let's
go to Bahia." It is crucial for us all to go together. But
you don't like Umbanda, you are Catholic. I love what
I know about your family. A breath of belonging. My
sister thinks it's crazy I don't know them. I'm a little nervous. My stomach is a little queasy. It is pretty cold here.
I wonder if you'll be able to handle it one day. Like what
if you move here. The photo lab and people working
there will miss you. They need to pay you more. Selling
equipment is hard work. You're too good for them, anyways. You're the greatest thrill and I know you. Why do
people value people when they are so-called successful?
Like potential is clear to vision. I see it kilometres away,
good dives into all ocean water. Please keep us in touch.
I know you will. I'm more secure than ever before. All
the negative feminists were a bit too hard. Just excuse
them. Many of their fathers cheated on their mothers,
or their exes cheated on them, or the women just could
not be happy. Relations were a blow too often, they for-

got about unconditional love and truth. I can't listen to these women. They will hate what I'm doing. They will think I need to ditch you fast. This will be my sister's first time going to Umbanda. I'll ask the avó if it's a good idea that you meet my sister. We'll see what she'll say. My sister will force it so we all meet. So cool, we can go for another swim. We can adventure. Our mind is made up. It's super real. We meeting into each other. We take more, give even more to others by us. We are slow together, yet we know we have a future.

Camila takes me to what she researched online. I could join the usual group, but here is some new beginning with her and me. I never examined this cactus so well, now this aloe vera plant. They are so strong with their juices inside. The pricks are just a face for such inner beauty. They are protective, you know. And for these reasons. Family is such a blessed space.

February 2, Iemenjá starts. And I know by the ocean the feeling is grandiose. Here sister is happy, and really that's all I want for her. She is akin to the avó here. There's that overwhelming feeling of self-doubt again. Like a choice to carry through a life with Zé could be the most practical mistake ever. A lie happens when cash meets our bridges. An alteration of design. If thinking too much on the go, the goal distorts itself. If there's one thing I always read from time to time, it's this: keep it all together. It's a little suspicious here. And moreover, I'm pretending to like it here, and I cannot leave. I grew up sleeping with my sister in her bed and for this trip, again we'll share a bed. I'm the kinda woman that can disappear to realize. Disappear to make myself known. I see this avó talking with my sister. My turn next. I always remember others' errors, and seldom will I not forgive. Sometimes families confused. Like status becomes some fake glue we cannot adhere to. Zé, your family is sacred. This avó here tells me you have a wife. That you've been lying to me. You know I don't trust this Umbanda anymore. I wanted antiquity's gossip, but modern was everywhere. Something more traditional, please. Don't get me wrong; I'm thankful for what I've always known. And it's because of you, I go on.

Camila slipped some cash for the avó. To break Phila from Zé. Camila had an idea that this particular Umbanda group was fake. Everyone knows an avó would never lie to make a profit, never lie period. It's only intuition and the orixás that they speak from. Camila knew they were in it for the money. That they were in it to take advantage of those who are down on their luck. Before the party gathering started, Camila went to the Umbanda home. Phila was still hanging out at their cousin's place. She knocked on the door. A young girl answered. She looked withdrawn but was forcing warmth and hospitality to come from her being and welcomed Camila inside. Camila asked frankly, "May I speak with the avó?" "My avó?" the girl asked. "I guess . . . the avó that will be here for this Iemenjá tonight." "Alright . . . I think she's resting, but I'll ask her . . . please sit." The girl pointed to the sofa by the entrance of the living area. Camila sat for a about ten minutes. She wasn't nervous at all. She knew she would get her wish. Her sister would never move to São Paulo. She would never leave the family. She would stay close with them. The avó came out of the bedroom wearing loose, light-coloured clothing. "Yes." "Here." Camila showed 1,000 reals. "I need you to tell my sister that her boyfriend has a wife." "Hmmm . . ." the avó said, staring at the money.

Family wants always what they feel is best for each member. Phila is often on her own quest, Camila is always trying to join, to connect, to keep up. Phila is always going to her sister when things go wrong. A sister panacea. But this time for Phila, there is no feeling of wrong. Camila cannot understand why Phila does not need her.

Heart

Zé and Phila, February and March 2016, São Paulo

But what about what the heart knows? Beauty as vulnerability's gesture. We walked to the park. Why is there only one door for an entrance and exit? As if we are the same beings while exiting as we were when we entered. Why cancel an appointment two hours after the appointment was made? Maybe organize another crime or two. Everybody knows. There's no point in being secretive. The stress to keep safe keeps people all together. And it would really suck if we didn't believe in change. The stress of tomorrow, we're not sure if we'll lose our jobs. But we will never lose each other. We grip our hands tightly together. We move through the busy crowd passively as we are not in any rush. As we are walking, we wanna love each and every one of you. And we, we don't mind, that's how we like each other, as long as we don't touch any other being, just touch each other. We are always celebrating our independence from status. And just because you do something bad to us doesn't mean we'll do it back to you. We don't believe in this kinda utilitarianism. A sister is often forgiven, a mother-in-law's love is sometimes won. First and foremost, we are lovers of good families with stories. We know we were born into our families for a reason. We contract simultaneously, not communicating directly like the atria and ventricles of the heart. To see all spaces together, but see them differently. We respect our visions off by heart. The strongest muscle, no economic system can destroy. Sometimes people can get ugly, you know. Going through a phase detoxifying the grime. Clogged arteries are not a time for us. Scheduling caesarians like business meetings, a neglect to have our order, looking people up and down to secure some sense of confidence. A kind of system we scoff to be a part of. That we are prophets in clean old clothing. The oxygen-rich blood going to the left side of the heart gets dispersed though our bodies. As we pulsate such might greater than the mind. Be careful what you project here. A thirty-three-year marriage with little heart and the woman struggling with varicose veins is no mightier than a divorce. Let's take our second shower together today. Let's allow for our midnight motel visits to continue. Let's allow for our: where are you? Who are you with? Send me a photo right now. Our cute jealousy flourish. So much heart lets this all continue. We take one stride at a beat, not thinking too much about next week. If we are caught with bad credit, so it is for our spontaneity. Let the education of your family always be our blessing, we can't believe in this anymore firmly. Things like forgiveness, empathy and genuine giving are fear liberated from advance. There's no need for a calculator while knowing many things by heart.

      The skyscrapers here are Tetris. The fractured fathers are left silent when their daughters speak wisdom they never wanted them to know. Or never wanted them to be able to utter. But we're birthed into what comforts and can defy us. We never escape. The heart it takes to say what it feels. It's not for show. During the news on the radio, there was talk of crimes of passion. If I can't have her, no one will, on repeat. Treat your children well, was announced after the talk of crimes of passion. And we're never afraid of what can happen. We and only we can be the best protectors of our family. Not any social assistance nor any counsellor. Spontaneity is more open than chance. Giorgio Agamben says spirituality is penetrating into things that any kinda self is lost being exposed. They don't want to see we've changed because they've tried to stuff us into a class system. We're not attached to items, not in our grace. We've always been able to see each other. Rain puddles turn into ideas we walk though. When family members come home with the stress of the day, we either ingest complaints or we all move into the next room, it all depends on the mood of the group for the moment. But always are we each others' pericardia. The comedy television show becomes where we can discuss later, laugh together now and view what is the blueprint for the jobs we may have where we sell products with co-workers laughing. But when the boss comes around, can we ever work. We are not full of anger. We are not giving up. We are in love with our families. We are not naively happy. We make others happy and because of this, we are happy.

We enter the metro together. Mass

crowds of people. A man screams just before two gunshots fire. People pushing, screaming, shoving. Mothers with their children. Two women yell, one after the other, "My purse." A man runs out of the metro clenching two bags. And all of us here at the metro station, some consoling the women, others sticking firmly to their mothers, to their lovers, to their children, to the very person standing right beside them. An announcement is made that the next train is running late.

Acknowledgments

Cover art credit due to Charles Venzon for concept and Sofia Lopes-Venzon for the cool heart illustration.

Much thanks to Malcolm Sutton for very astute editorial suggestions and for believing in the project.

Thanks to Angela Carr, Juliana Spahr and Oana Avasilichioaei, who all read the work with very attentive eyes.

Linda Kallon and family for serving the world as an example of what hospitality truly is. A loyal warrior friend. African queen.

Linda Chen for your rich inner workings and depth of vision of the human condition.

Kaya Fukuda for filling our home with your gracious femininity.

Viviane Gabriela Baptista, uma mulher incredible. Você é tão forte e fiel.

Thanks to my parents and brother and sister-in-law and family for always being the practical voice of life.

Thanks to the Venzon family.

Thanks to the Mesquita family.

Thanks to the Lopes family.

Cherry Cervantes for our hang-out sessions with our darlings and great dialogues.

Kamal Daisy Bedi for our dear friendship, over sixteen years of getting philosophical.

Daniel Matshine Obrigada pra me ensinar mais do luz preto. Saudades de nossos conversos na universidade.

Cam Scott for our long walks and talks under the bridge.

Colin Smith for your profound friendship and editorial attention. Many days walking and conversing served as panaceas during dreary times.

Theo Simms for our friendship and many mornings with good coffee and intense dialogues.

Marco Castillo for our Virgo sifting discussions of the world.

Raul Pazos and Jose Inle Ladeira for your friendship and for sharing your apartment where most of this manuscript was written. Obrigada com o fundo de meu coração. Seu apartamento foi sempre aberto e cheio de boa énergia.

Tara Mooney for our many days with children and long, dearly friendship.

Greatest love to my divinities: Sofia and Giovanna, living a matriarchal way replete with unconditional love.

For Marcio Mesquita for our rhythmic spontaneity and carinho e amor.

For Deus.

Colophon

Distributed in Canada by the Literary Press Group:
www.lpg.ca

Distributed in the United States by Small Press Distribution:
www.spdbooks.org

Shop online at www.bookthug.ca

Designed by Malcolm Sutton
Edited for the press by Malcolm Sutton
Copy edited by Ruth Zuchter

BOOK
PRODUCTION
WAR ECONOMY
STANDARD